We live here

THE TALES OF
WYLDE ACRE WOOD

BOOK ONE

The Becky Falls Adventure &
Brad and Ron Take to the Air

Written by Gerald Dunn
Illustrated by Baz

Gerald Dunn (signature)

DramWorks

ISBN 978-0-9570775-3-9

FOREWORD

Like a lot of Dads, Gerald made up bedtime stories for his daughter, Katie, while she was growing up at their home in the Devon countryside. During a period of working in the Forest of Dean he became close friends with Baz, a local artist, and was hugely impressed by his amazing drawings. From this friendship Wylde Acre Wood was born; a fictitious amalgam of Dartmoor and the Forest of Dean. These first two stories introduce the main characters, Brad and Ron, but they only scratch the surface of a much bigger and complex woodland community. Hopefully more of the many stories they have written and illustrated together will appear in print soon.

THE
BECKY FALLS
ADVENTURE

CHAPTER ONE

Deep in a badger sett in Wylde Acre Wood, Brad Badger was wide awake reading a book. This was unusual for Brad, as during the holidays he normally went to bed late and got up very late. Today was different. Brad and his best friend, Ron Rabbit, had been building a raft at Becky Falls and today they were planning to sail it for the first time. Brad and Ron loved playing around with water. One of their favourite pastimes was building a dam across one of the many streams that flowed out of the lake at Becky Falls. They tried to see how much water they could hold back before the dam broke, which it always did. Brad looked at his clock again. Twenty to seven. Even his dad wouldn't be out of bed yet. Brad sneaked into the kitchen, made himself a cup of tea and took it back to bed. Yes, today was very different. This was the first time he had ever done anything in the kitchen except eat. On the dot of seven, Brad ran back into the kitchen and found his mother cooking breakfast.

CHAPTER TWO

Breakfast was normally a pleasant and relaxed time in the badger household, but not this morning. *It's so unfair!"* wailed Belinda, Brad's younger sister. *"Brad is going out without me, the selfish pig."* Tears streamed down her cheeks.

"*Chill out, Belly!"* grinned Brad. Using that nickname always made her furious.

"*Be quiet the pair of you!"* roared Mr Badger, glaring over the top of his newspaper. "*The first day of the school holidays and you're squabbling already."* Belinda stomped off and slammed her bedroom door behind her. Secretly she was very fond of Ron Rabbit and had been looking forward to a day out with him and Brad. She couldn't believe that Brad could be so cruel. How she hated him.

"*Girls!"* muttered Brad under his breath in the next room.

CHAPTER THREE

Mrs Badger said "*Now make sure you both take care,*" as she handed Brad his packed lunch. "*The wood can be a very dangerous place.*"

"Don't worry, mum," laughed Brad. "*Ron and I are nearly a year old now and quite grown up.*"

"I dare say," said his mother, "*but that dreadful fox has been seen around recently and the rivers are very dangerous. There's been a lot of rain in the last few weeks.*"

"Ferdy Fox doesn't eat badgers!" Brad continued, still laughing, "*and Ron and I are the best swimmers in our class at school.*" Actually that wasn't quite true and Brad felt guilty as he said it. Both Ron and Brad struggled with their swimming and Ron still needed water wings.

"Ferdy may not eat badgers," warned Mrs Badger, "*but he does eat rabbits and just you remember what happened to Ron's young sisters.*"

Brad shivered. Ron's three youngest sisters were missing, presumed eaten. Ron had never been the same since they had disappeared and refused to talk about it.

"OK mum, we'll be careful," said Brad sadly, wishing quietly that his best friend could be a badger and not a vulnerable rabbit. "*We'll be back before dark,*" he added and scampered out of the door towards the large rock where he always met his friend.

CHAPTER FOUR

When Brad got to the rock he found Ron waiting for him. "*Hi Brad!*" shouted Ron as he bounded towards Brad excitedly. "*Where's Bel? Isn't she coming with us?*" he asked, now looking rather disappointed.

"*No,*" replied Brad. "*She wanted to come but I told her it was a boys-only adventure. She was really pathetic and cried like a baby.*" Ron fell silent. He wasn't very fond of most girls but he thought Belinda was the prettiest, most delightful animal he had ever met.

"*What's up with you?*" asked Brad. "*Would you rather sail the raft with my sister?*" He laughed and Ron felt very uncomfortable. But the

question wasn't answered, because just at that moment they heard a loud noise coming from the oak tree above them. It was Oleander the owl. Oleander was a strange but wise old bird and seemed to know everything that was going on in the wood. The strangest thing of all was that whilst he hooted at night like a normal owl, during the day he spoke in rhyme.

"*What a lovely sunny day,*
  Where are you two off to play?"

he hooted loudly.

Brad jumped. He had thought he was alone with Ron so he was rather annoyed to find that someone might have been listening to their conversation. He glared at the old owl. Oleander glared back but Brad knew it was only his huge eyes that made him seem fierce and that really he was a very friendly bird. Under the owl's wing was a big book which Oleander called the "Book of Everything." He referred to it when the other animals of the Wood asked him questions, which they very often did.

Quickly getting over his frustration, Brad replied cheerfully, "*Hello Olly! Ron and I are off to Becky Falls. We've been building a raft down there and today we're taking her out for the first time.*"

"Do be careful, I'm never wrong,
The currents there are very strong!"

warned the old owl.

"*You worry too much,*" laughed Ron, forgetting his earlier embarrassment now. "*Come on Brad, let's get going.*"

CHAPTER FIVE

The troubles that were going to meet them that warm summer day started around the first corner. Lying on the ground in front of them was poor old Mrs Squirrel. She was holding her ankle and groaning. She hadn't noticed the boys yet and Brad leaned in to whisper to Ron. "*Shall we sneak by behind those trees? If we stay and help we'll waste hours of precious time.*"

"*We can't do that!*" hissed Ron. "*It will break every rule of the Forest Convention.*"

"*The Forest what?*" asked Brad, puzzled.

"*The woodland rules,*" said Ron. "*Don't you ever listen in school?*" Brad actually spent most of his time in school staring out of the window and didn't really care much about rules and regulations anyway. "*Come on,*" said Ron. "*We've got to help. Think about what happened to my sisters.*" It was the first time that Ron had mentioned his sisters since that

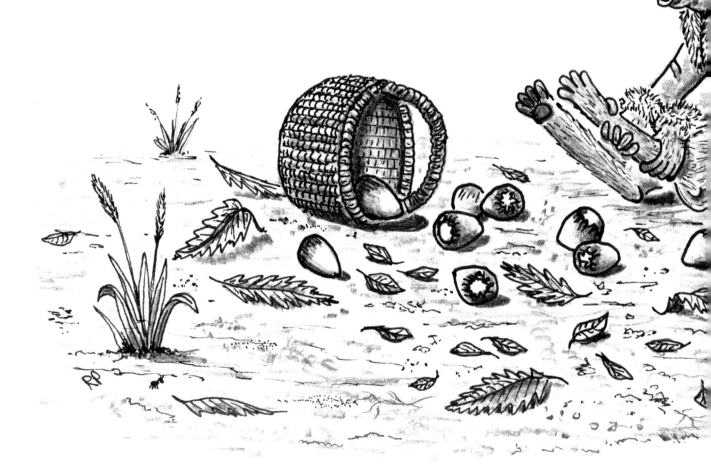

tragic day and this shocked Brad into action. He talked to Mrs Squirrel while Ron picked up the nuts lying all over the ground and put them back in her basket.

"*I've been here for ages,*" she moaned. "*I tripped over that root and I think I've broken my ankle. Do you think you could help me back to Drey Cottage?*" Ron noticed Brad's annoyed look. Drey Cottage was at least a mile away in the wrong direction.

"*Of course,*" said Brad and Ron together. With difficulty they helped Mrs Squirrel up. She put her arms around their shoulders and they started on the long, tedious journey to her home.

CHAPTER SIX

The boys came to the conclusion that Mrs Squirrel had eaten more than her fair share of nuts during her lifetime. The further they got, the heavier she seemed to become. At long last Drey Cottage came into view and they could see Doc Squirrel running to meet them.

"*Sheila! What's happened?*" asked Doc, looking very concerned. Mrs Squirrel told her husband the story. He smiled at the boys and patted Brad on the back.

"*Thank you very much for your help, boys. I shall be telling your parents how brilliant you've been,*" he said, still smiling. "*Come in! Come in and have some tea and biscuits.*"

It was very fortunate that he was the woodland doctor as Mrs Squirrel's ankle was indeed broken. Doc assured her that he would be able to mend and bandage it straight away.

CHAPTER SEVEN

D rey Cottage was an interesting place set high in the top of an extremely tall tree. It was easily accessible by nimble squirrels in full health but not by a badger, a rabbit and an old squirrel with a damaged ankle. Fortunately there was a winch on the porch, normally used for hauling up provisions in a basket. Doc Squirrel ran up the tree and then winched the other three up, one at a time.

Brad was rather heavy and Doc Squirrel struggled with the winch handle. By the time Brad reached the top the Doc was doubled over, gasping for breath.

"*Should be easier on the way down,*" he laughed.

Brad got out of the basket and then made the mistake of looking down. He gasped and then felt dizzy. The Doc had to grab his arm to stop him from falling off the edge of the porch. Brad and Ron were not at all used to heights and felt extremely nervous, even when they were safely inside the cottage and sitting down. The whole building was moving even though there was hardly any wind. Doc Squirrel made the tea and then set to work on Mrs Squirrel's ankle. Ron asked if they ever got seasick when the wind got up. Mrs Squirrel admitted that it could get a bit rocky and that in serious storms everything needed to be tied down for safety. She thanked them again for their help. Brad felt rather guilty that his first reaction had been to slip by without helping, but he smiled when he thought about someone saying nice things about him to his parents. Normally it was just the opposite, as Brad did seem to get into rather a lot of trouble.

Brad soon ran out of things to say but he was impressed with Ron's confident conversational skills. Ron asked after the squirrels' elder children, Cyril and Sheryl, who were schoolmates with Brad and Ron. Mrs Squirrel explained that the children were staying with their cousins in the Deep Wood for a while. When they eventually finished their tea and biscuits, Doc Squirrel asked them where they had been going when they had first met his wife. They told him about Becky Falls and the doctor smiled.

"*I've got a surprise for you,*" he said. "*Follow me.*"

CHAPTER EIGHT

Once they had reached ground level again, after a scary descent in the basket, they were led down a path behind the tree to a garden shed. Inside was an old motorbike and sidecar. Doc Squirrel was evidently proud of his bike as it gleamed like a new pin. *"He must polish it every day,"* the boys thought.

"*Let's take her for a spin,*" laughed Doc. Ron had the feeling that it was going to be a rather fast spin and Doc Squirrel did not disappoint him. In fact it was so fast that Ron spent most of the journey with his paws over his eyes. He was glad to be in the sidecar where he could crouch down. He was sure that at times Brad actually left the saddle and only stayed on by grabbing the squirrel's tail. Half way through the journey they came across the weasel family, out for a stroll. Nobody in the wood cared much for the weasels. The parents were horrible and the two twin sons, Wally and Wayne, were just downright nasty. The twins had come close to being expelled from school many times for bullying, but

unfortunately they were still there. The motorbike was going so fast now that the weasels had little time to get out of the way. In a flurry of leaves they all dived into the ditch to avoid the spinning wheels.

When Brad looked back he could see Wally and Wayne pointing. He knew they had spotted him. Luckily, school was still six weeks away.

"*They might forget,*" thought Brad, but deep down he knew they wouldn't.

CHAPTER NINE

Becky Falls was a beautiful place. Water cascaded over rocks and thundered into a deep lake causing a fine mist to drift across the water. Dragonflies skimmed the surface and wild rabbits gambolled around on the grassy banks leading down to the water's edge. Several stood still and stared, hardly believing their eyes when they saw a much bigger rabbit standing on its hind legs and carrying rocks and sticks. Brad and Ron were building a dam.

There were several small streams flowing out of the lake and they enjoyed blocking up one of them to see how big a pond they could make. Eventually the water pressure would be so much that the dam would break and then they would try somewhere else. A very friendly bird called Ken Fisher helped them. He couldn't carry much except a few twigs, but it all helped and he enjoyed himself very much.

After a while, Brad and Ron sat down and munched some sandwiches. They discussed what they would do with their raft. It was finished now, apart from one corner where the logs were a bit loose. They spent the next half hour lashing these together with some strong rope.

"*I'm still not happy with that corner,*" fussed Ron.

"*It'll have to do,*" snapped Brad, "*because I can't wait any longer to launch her.*" They moved the raft to the edge of water. "*I name this ship HMS Bark Royal,*" shouted Brad, saluting. Then he threw some lemonade over it to complete the naming ceremony. Ron laughed. Brad was mad but great fun and a very good friend. They pushed the raft into the water and jumped on, holding their breath. She floated and they cheered excitedly.

CHAPTER TEN

At first all was well. They paddled happily around the large lake, splashing each other rather a lot. But then they got closer to where the main waterfall cascaded into the lake. Brad suddenly noticed that the current was pulling them towards it.

"*Quick!*" he shouted. "*Paddle as hard as you can away from the waterfall.*" But, as hard as they paddled, they could not break free from the strong current. Brad had to make a quick decision, swim for it or stay with the raft. He chose to stay, as he knew that they were both poor swimmers. At least if they stayed with the raft they would have something to hold on to. Ron started to squeak with fright. Soon Brad could not even hear Ron's squeaking because of the noise. The water looked like a boiling cauldron and spray was hitting their faces very hard. They both lay down flat and held on for dear life. Then the water hit them with tremendous force.

The corner of the raft that they had just been working on could not take the strain and it broke away. Unfortunately, Ron was holding onto it and the boys were pulled in different directions. Ron went down and down, into the depths. He held both his log and his breath for dear life, but this was the end. He knew it. His life flashed before his eyes: his warm burrow, his mum and dad, Belinda, Rita his only remaining sister, the other sisters he had lost and his best friend, Brad, who would now surely drown with him. It was over. But then, all of a sudden, he realised that he could hear again. His head was above the water and he gasped for breath. He had made it!

Slowly, he opened his eyes and saw that he was on a sandy beach in a cave behind the waterfall. All thoughts about his dice with death left his head as he gasped, *"Treasure!"*
In all the stories he had ever read about places behind waterfalls, there was always treasure.

He jumped up, pulled his life-saving log onto the beach and started to explore his surroundings. Disappointingly, there were no chests of treasure bursting with gems but at the back of the cave there was a round hole leading into a tunnel. Ron bravely popped his head into the hole but it was pitch black and didn't smell very pleasant. He quickly pulled it out again and at that moment he thought about Brad. He rushed to the beach. There was only one thing he could do. He grabbed his log and plunged back into the turbulent water.

CHAPTER ELEVEN

Ron was buffeted this way and that by the force of the water. Every part of his body hurt. His lungs were bursting, but finally his head popped up out of the water on the right side of the waterfall. He kicked his legs frantically to push himself away from the thundering water. He had made it! A big smile came to his face when he looked towards the bank. There was the broken raft and standing beside it was Brad, with his head in his hands, looking at the ground and wiping big tears from his eyes. As Ron got closer, he could hear Brad crying, *"Oh Ron! I've killed you! However will I tell your parents?"*

"Tell them what!" shouted Ron. Brad looked up and couldn't believe his eyes. He jumped up, plunged back into the water and swam over to Ron. *"Ron! I thought you were, were…"*

"Well! I'm not," said Ron, *"and I've got some very exciting news."* Brad gave Ron a huge hug and helped him back to the bank. *"I'm starving!"* said Ron, so they sat down to eat the rest of their sandwiches and tell each other everything that had happened. Brad had been lucky. He had held onto the raft like a limpet. The raft had been pushed under the water but it had popped back up like a cork and floated into the middle of the lake. Brad had stayed looking into

the water for ages but had eventually given up all hope of ever seeing Ron again. They laughed and joked and soon the very close shave became part of the exciting adventure they were having. Now they were only thinking about treasure.

"*There's only one way back in,*" said Brad, shuddering. "*That log saved my life,*" said Ron. "*I don't think a big log like that could ever sink.*" The plan was hatched. They would strap themselves to large logs using rope and brave the thundering waters of Becky Falls again. This was the bravest thing that Ron had ever done in his life and Brad was proud of him. They pushed off from the bank. Ron's heart was beating fast as they approached the boiling waters.

And then they were in…

CHAPTER TWELVE

They both popped up on the other side of the waterfall at the same moment. "*We've done it!*" shouted Brad, as they quickly untied themselves from their logs.

"*How will we get the treasure out?*" asked Ron.

"*Don't worry about that yet,*" said Brad. "*Let's find it first.*"

They explored the cave again but found nothing on the surface. Maybe it was buried, they thought, so they started to dig like mad. Sand went flying but they soon sat down exhausted, realising there was nothing there. Then their eyes turned to the tunnel. "*We've got to go in,*" said Brad. "*I tell you what. You go first, Ron, and I'll guard us from the back.*"

"*Not likely!*" squeaked Ron. "*I found the place. It's your turn now.*"

35

"*OK,*" agreed Brad, "*we'll take it in turns. Follow me.*" They tiptoed quietly into the dark tunnel. It was just high enough for them to stand upright but only wide enough for one of them at a time. It was level for quite a while but then it turned a corner and started to go down.

"*I've got a bad feeling about this,*" moaned Ron. "*What if something big and ugly lives down here?*" Brad hadn't thought about that.

"*Too late now,*" he said. "*Do come along and stop moaning.*" As they turned yet another corner, a nasty smell hit their nostrils.

"*Ugggh! What on earth is that smell?*" asked Ron, holding his nose. Suddenly Brad called out as he stepped on something sharp. He picked up the something and examined it with his paw. There wasn't enough light to see, but he could feel what it was.

"*Fish bones!*" exclaimed Brad.

"*Fish bones!*" squeaked Ron. "*That means something lives down here that eats fish!*" Suddenly a large shape moved in front of them and a strange chilling voice hissed, "*Who dares enter my tunnel uninvited?*" The boys had never been so frightened in their lives.

"*Run for it!*" shouted Brad and they both ran as fast as their short legs could carry them, towards the dim light at the end of the tunnel. Ron tripped and Brad fell over him. They could hear the noise of something absolutely enormous following them. They picked themselves up quickly and ran on again. At last they reached the cave and, without looking back, they both plunged headlong into the water.

36

CHAPTER THIRTEEN

Down and down they sank and Brad knew that this must be the end of them both. Without the logs there was no hope of getting back to the surface. But if they had stayed in the cave any longer, the monster in the tunnel would surely have caught them.

What a mess. Why hadn't they just gone home the first time? He couldn't hold his breath for much longer. Suddenly he felt a firm grip on his arm and realised that he was being pulled upwards.

"*It can't be Ron,*" he thought and then everything went black.

The next thing he knew, he was coughing and spluttering on the bank and there beside him was Ron doing exactly the same thing.

"*Well, well! Ronald Rabbit and Bradley Badger. I might have guessed.*" Standing over them was Oscar the otter, grinning from ear to ear. "*Guess I frightened you boys a little, eh?*" he chuckled. The two boys nodded.

"*So! Someone has discovered my holt at last,*" he said.

"*Holt?*" asked Ron.

"*A holt is an otter's home,*" said Oscar, "*and until today, no-one in the Wood had any idea where I lived.*" Oscar was a very private person and the whereabouts of his home had always been a big mystery in the woodland community.

"*We won't tell anyone!*" squeaked Ron, "*will we Brad?*"

"*No, Oscar,*" said Brad shaking. "*We promise.*"

"*Never been to my swimming lessons have you, boys?*" said Oscar. The boys shook their heads. "*Every youngster needs to be a strong*

swimmer," said Oscar, "*especially in a wood with so many rivers and lakes. Today's adventure could have had a very different ending and just think how sad your parents and siblings would have been then.*"

"*Thank you very much for rescuing us, Oscar,*" said Brad. "*We've been pretty silly haven't we, Ron?*" Ron nodded silently.

"*I'll tell you what,*" said Oscar. "*If you promise to come to my swimming lessons each week and to keep the location of my home a secret, I'll promise not to tell your parents anything about what happened here today. What do you say?*" Oscar held out his paw and Brad and Ron shook it eagerly in agreement. If their parents had found out that they had nearly drowned, they would probably have been grounded for the rest of the holiday, or worse. "*Well! I'd better get back to my family,*" said Oscar. "*Monday morning, ten o'clock and don't be late,*" and with that he dived gracefully back into the water.

"*We'll be there!*" shouted the boys.

"*Brrrr, I'm getting cold,*" said Brad. He opened his backpack and took out his towel.

"*Your mum thinks of everything,*" said Ron, enviously. He started to shiver.

"*Here, have the towel and wrap it around yourself,*" said Brad. "*Well! I've had enough for one day. Shall we head for home?*"

"*Yes. Let's go,*" said Ron, shouldering his backpack.

CHAPTER FOURTEEN

I'm home, Mum," shouted Brad as he came through the front door of the sett. "*You're back early dear,*" she said. "*Is everything all right?*"

"*Couldn't be better,*" said Brad, "*what's for tea?*"

"*Lizard soup with slug tart for dessert,*" his mum answered.

"*Yum, slug tart, my favourite,*" said Brad. "*Is Bel here?*"

"*Yes, she's in her room but she's still a bit grumpy with you, so look out,*" warned Mrs Badger.

Brad knocked on Belinda's door. "*Can I come in, Sis?*" he said.

"*Get lost!*" shouted Belinda crossly, but Brad opened the door anyway.

"*Look!*" he said, "*I'm really sorry we went without you today. Would you like to come with us next time?*" She jumped up and smiled.

"*Yes please! Where are you going tomorrow?*"

"*Tomorrow I'm going to stay home and play with you,*" he said. Mrs Badger was listening to all of this and she couldn't believe her ears.

"*Either Brad is going down with some terrible illness, or something happened today that he's not telling me about,*" she thought. "*I'll find out what it is.*" But Mrs Badger never did find out what had happened and to this day, the whereabouts of Oscar the otter's holt is still a mystery in Wylde Acre Wood… except to two young adventurers.

BRAD AND RON TAKE TO THE AIR

CHAPTER ONE

Brad Badger was bored. It was the middle of the summer holidays. His sister Belinda was staying with their grandmother in the Deep Wood and he and his friend, Ron Rabbit, had run out of new and interesting things to do.

"*Go and help your dad,*" suggested his mother, turning from the slugs she was cooking. "*He and Ron's father are mending the old foot bridge down at Thorny Bottom.*"

"No thanks," moaned Brad. "*I don't fancy mixing concrete and carrying stones in this hot weather.*" "Suit yourself," said his mother sternly, wagging her finger at him, "*but I don't want you hanging around here all day, moaning and getting under my feet. Anyway,*" she said, looking at the clock, "*it's nearly time for you to go and meet Ronald.*"

47

CHAPTER TWO

Brad and Ron always met at ten o'clock under the oak tree next to the big rock. Oleander the owl was usually sitting in the tree and today was no exception.

"Tu-whit tu-whoo, what's the matter with you?
Your faces are long and so sad,
There's plenty to see, there's plenty to do,
It really cannot be that bad."

he hooted.

"*It's worse than bad,*" said Brad. "*What can we do Olly?*"

Now, Oleander was a wise old owl and always carried a book under his wing called the Book of Everything. He leafed through the book for a few minutes and finally he hooted:

"What can we do with bored children like you
On a day that is windy and bright,
My book never lies, on this page it describes
How much fun can be had with a kite."

"*A kite!*" Ron grinned. "*Does it tell you how to make one, Olly?*"
Oleander flew down to the ground with the open book. Ron took a pen and paper from his rucksack and scribbled down the instructions. "*We need some sticks, rope and an old sheet,*" he said to Brad. "*I know where to get those,*" whispered Brad, winking at Ron. "*Follow me!*" They thanked Oleander for his help and dashed off into the woods.

CHAPTER THREE

Soon they arrived at a secret place, known only to some of the animal children in the wood. They called it "Location X" and it was a mysterious cave, with its entrance hidden by thick ivy and bushes. If any of the children found anything interesting in the forest or by the big road, usually junk left behind by humans, they would bring it to Location X and store it for later use. Brad pushed back the bushes and the boys entered the dark cave. Before long they reappeared with a length of rope and an old sheet which they had used before as the sail on their raft. They had also found a handsaw and they set to work straight away by cutting down some sticks.

CHAPTER FOUR

R *ight! Get out the instructions!"* ordered Brad and so Ron laid out his notes on the floor. His writing was very untidy and there were dirty paw prints everywhere. Brad found it difficult to read some of the words. *"This says it's a hundred somethings long by fifty somethings wide."* Ron looked puzzled. *"It looks like 'centipedes'!"* Brad said, staring at a word obscured by a large paw print.

"*How long is a centipede?"* asked Ron.

"*We'll have to catch one,"* said Brad and he started snuffling about among the leaves on the forest floor. After a while he found an enormous centipede. It was not at all happy at being captured and it wriggled and writhed until Brad threatened to eat it if it didn't keep still. After that, it behaved perfectly and soon they had cut a stick to the exact length of the centipede. Using this as their measure, they were able to get to work and follow the instructions in Ron's notes. The boys had great fun building their new kite and the insect was delighted to find that they were taking no more notice of it, so it quickly scuttled off into the bushes.

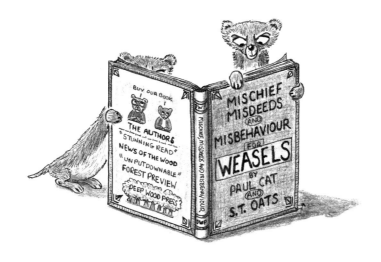

CHAPTER FIVE

When they had finished, they stood back to admire their work. "*It looks huge,*" said Brad. "*I've never seen a kite that big before.*" The boys did not realise, as you do, that the kite's measurements should have been in centimetres not centipedes and, as the centipede was five centimetres long, the kite was actually five times too big. "*Come on Ron!*" shouted Brad. "*Let's get up to Dizzy Heights and fly this thing.*"

"*OK, but let's go round by the brook,*" said Ron, "*because I don't want to bump into those nasty weasel twins.*"

"*Don't you worry about those two losers,*" said Brad. "*I can handle them.*"

So they set off along the road to Dizzy Heights. Unfortunately, as Ron knew, this road led straight past the weasels' home and sure enough there they were, skulking around outside in the garden.

"*Oh look!*" growled Wally, the biggest and nastiest of the twins. "*Here come Batman and Robin and what a pretty kite they've built.*"

"*Hee-hee-hee,*" sniggered Wayne, the second brother. Ron felt very uncomfortable but Brad soon had the situation under control.

"*Don't be nasty to us or I'll ask my dad's friend Ferdy Fox to pay you a visit,*" said Brad.

"*All right, keep your fur on,*" squeaked Wally, obviously worried. Ferdy Fox really was the nastiest animal in the forest and in fact had no friends at all. The weasels scuttled off into the woods, much to Ron's relief. After that, the journey was uneventful and at last they reached the slopes leading up to the high peak of Dizzy Heights.

CHAPTER SIX

Climbing the steep slope was not easy at the best of times, but carrying a huge kite in a strong wind made it very difficult. Once or twice the wind nearly ripped the kite from their grasp but finally they staggered to the very top, completely out of breath. They sat for a while to recover and ate some of the lunch they had brought with them in their backpacks. The wind was getting stronger all the time and they had to sit on the kite to hold it down.

"You grab the tail rope and I'll hold the kite," said Brad at last. By this time the wind was howling and Brad was struggling to hold the kite down. Suddenly, there was a ferocious gust and the kite sailed into the air taking the unfortunate badger with it. Ron squeaked with fright and held onto the tail rope tightly. He had tied it to his arm to make absolutely sure it did not slip out of his grasp, but now it tightened and Ron was pulled violently into the air. Up went the kite and up went the boys, higher and higher, while they screamed for help. Soon Brad came to his senses and he shouted down to the terrified young rabbit dangling on the end of the rope.

"Climb up the rope, Ron!" It took a long time to get Ron to hear as he wouldn't stop shrieking, but finally he understood and started to climb. When he reached Brad, he grabbed onto the bar that Brad was holding. But this caused the kite to lurch violently to one side so Brad pushed him further away until the kite levelled up again. They were still climbing steeply and the trees in the forest seemed like tiny specks below them.

CHAPTER SEVEN

L*ean forward!*" shouted Brad and as they both leaned forward, the kite levelled out and then began to go down again. They soon found that by altering their position they could completely control the kite and then Brad began to enjoy himself.

Down and down they flew, heading back towards Dizzy Heights. Fortunately the peak was easy to spot as it poked through the sea of green trees far below them. Ron wanted to land straight away and walk home as he hated heights but Brad was enjoying himself too much.

"*This is turning into the best adventure of the holidays,*" he shouted. "*We can't land yet!*"

"*Oh, all right,*" moaned Ron as Brad shifted position and the kite headed towards home. Soon they were flying over Bubble Brook and Raven Spinney and suddenly Brad spotted two animals moving by the edge of the brook. Brad pointed and Ron shouted, "*It's those horrible weasel twins again.*" Brad's eyes twinkled as he turned the kite towards them. Down swooped the kite and at the last minute the weasels noticed its dark shadow on the ground and turned around. Brad and Ron started yelling at the tops their voices. "*Aagh!*" squealed the weasel twins in fright and they both fell backwards off the bank into the oozy mud far below. Poor Wally went in head first. What a mess. Brad and Ron soared back into the air, roaring with laughter. The twins were left far behind, shaking their fists and trying to scrape the smelly, sticky mud from their fur.

CHAPTER EIGHT

B rad turned the kite again. "*Where are we going now?*" groaned Ron. "*The Hedge of the Known World!*" shouted Brad. "*I want to see what's behind it.*" Ron gasped. No one knew what lay beyond the old hedge but there were many stories, most of them bad. The most famous was about the Raggedy Man. Rumour had it that if anyone saw the Raggedy Man, they would be turned to stone.

On they went, with Ron getting more and more agitated by the minute. Over the Lonely Oak and then over the Deep Quarry they flew until suddenly, there in the distance was the Hedge itself. Brad was excited. Ron had shut his eyes. Brad strained his eyes and was sure he could just make out the outline of a man surrounded by black birds. To his horror he realised that some of the birds were flying straight towards them. They were bigger than crows. They looked like ravens with huge, sharp black beaks.

"*I don't like this!*" cried Brad and he quickly turned the kite around and dived to pick up more speed. But the giant birds soon caught up with them and circled them menacingly. One dived at the kite and then several beaks broke through the sheet. There was a loud ripping sound and a large hole appeared down one side. The kite lurched to the left and started to spin out of control. As they plummeted, the birds flew off. By shifting their weight, the boys managed to pull the kite out of the dive and even gain some height but the kite was hard to control now and they felt that it might crash at any moment.

THE RAGGEDY MAN

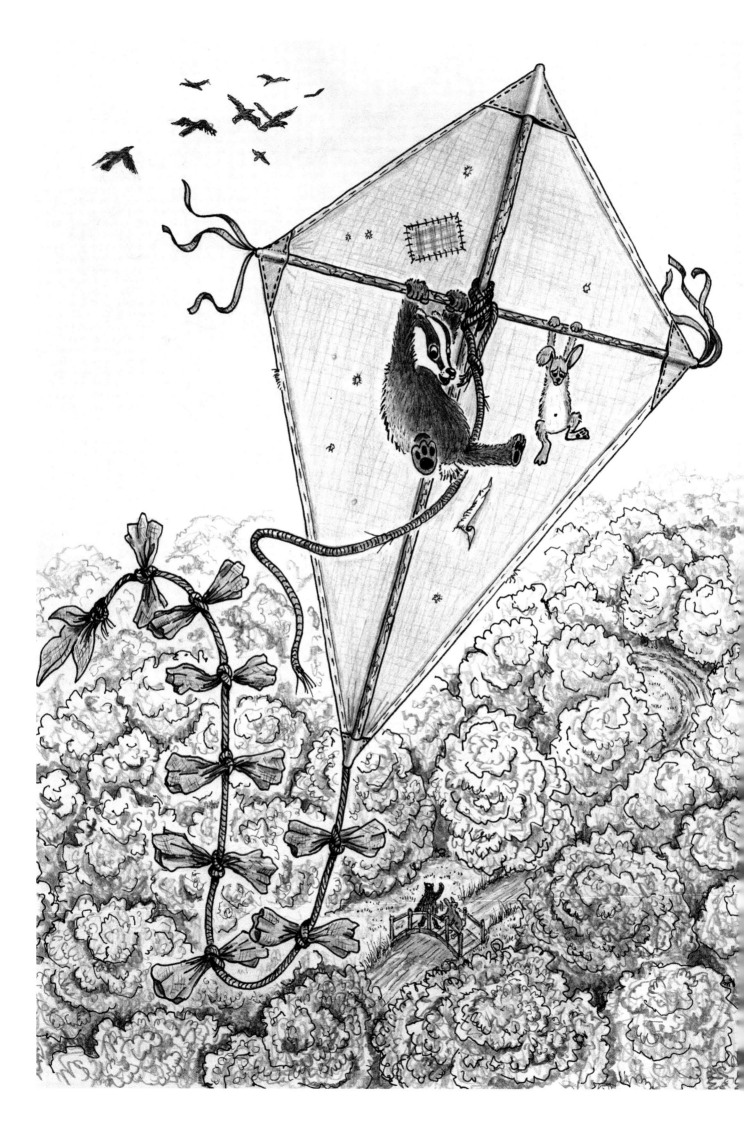

And then they had a stroke of luck. They realised that they were now flying over the footbridge at Thorny Bottom where Bill Badger and Rab Rabbit were working. "*Help!*" shouted the boys. Their fathers looked up and couldn't believe their eyes.

"*What on earth are those boys doing up there?*" exclaimed Bill Badger. He stared in disbelief at the kite, which was rocking violently from side to side with Brad and Ron hanging onto it for dear life.

"*Quick Rab, you try to follow them. I'll fetch Oleander. He'll know what to do.*" With that, Bill jumped on his bicycle and sped off down the track.

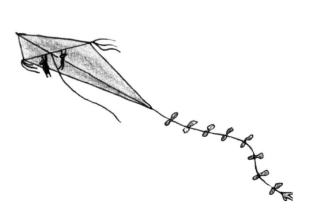

CHAPTER NINE

The next twenty minutes were the worst of Brad's life. He was tossed this way and then that way. He went soaring up and then plummeting down. He always felt that at any moment they would crash and worse than that, he felt sick. Ron was a gibbering wreck and couldn't even speak. Fortunately though, help was on the way. Bill Badger had found Oleander and the owl was flying as fast as he could to reach them. After what seemed like a lifetime, Brad felt that the kite had stabilised and was floating gently downwards. He looked up and saw that Oleander had his talons in the sheet from above and was controlling the descent. At last they came to earth smoothly in a clearing close to Brad's home. Many woodland creatures had gathered to

see the flying animals and they clapped and cheered as the kite landed. Brad's mother rushed over and hugged him, much to his embarrassment. Ron soon recovered when he was back on solid ground again and he began telling the story as if they had planned the whole thing. He even said that he had thoroughly enjoyed it. Brad laughed. Although the boys had been in a very dangerous situation, their parents knew that they had meant to fly the kite rather than be flown by it. So Brad and Ron didn't get told off, well not much anyway, and everyone was invited back to the badgers' sett for tea and cakes.

CHAPTER TEN

The next day, Brad and Ron were perfectly happy to help their fathers mend the old footbridge at Thorny Bottom. They both felt that they had had enough adventures for a day or two. Brad got a long lecture from his father about young animals keeping their feet on the ground. Brad argued that Mr Hare always delivered the post using a balloon. Bill pointed out that Mr Hare was an adult for one thing and that he had a pilot's licence for another.

¡CAUTION!
ANIMALS AT WORK
BROCK BUILDERS Cº

Actually, Brad and Ron didn't particularly want to go flying again anyway. It had all been a bit too frightening, if they were being perfectly honest. The weasel twins were secretly impressed by Brad and Ron's exploits and treated them much more respectfully after that. They even seemed to forget about the motorbike incident. The legend of the Raggedy Man grew and animal children were warned by their parents to stay well away from the Hedge of the Known World. Brad and Ron were treated like celebrities for the next few weeks and were asked to repeat the tale many, many times. As you can imagine, the tale grew longer and more incredible with each telling.

THE TALES OF WYLDE ACRE WOOD